How Are You?

¿Cómo estás?

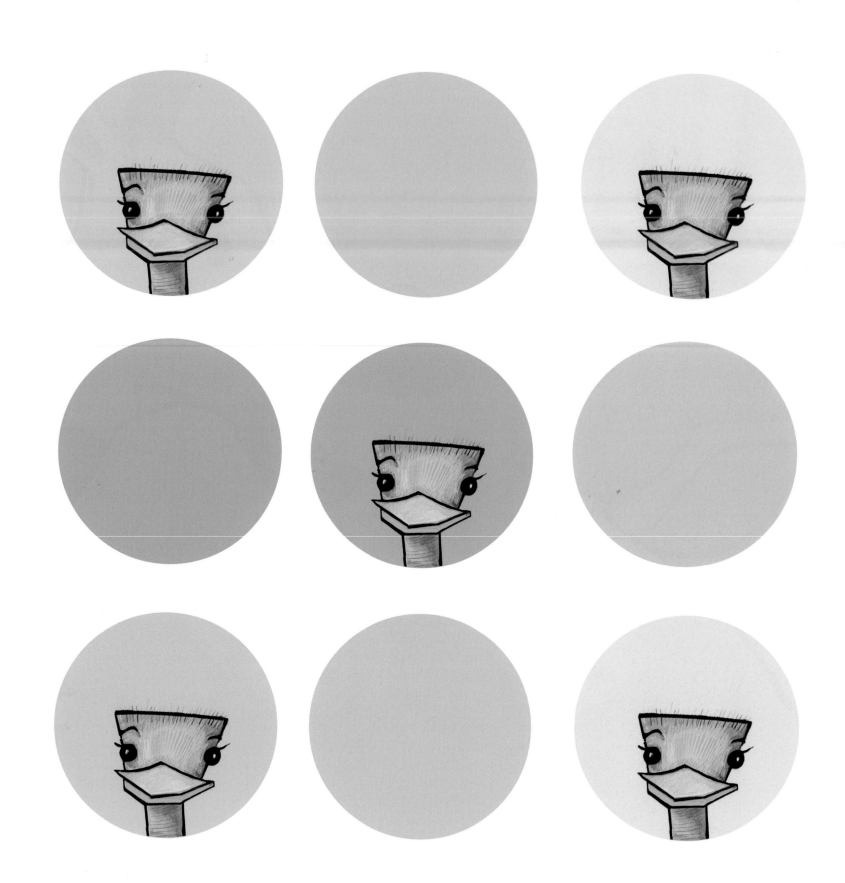

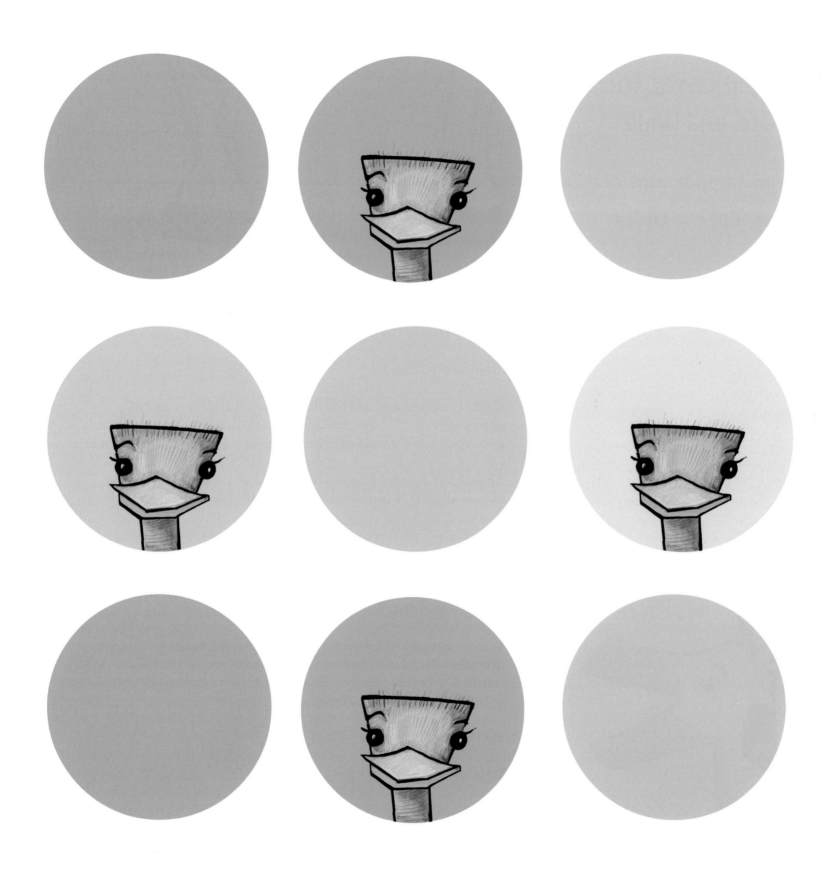

To my family, friends,
Kate, and Linda

Para mi familia, mis
amigos, Kate y Linda

Originally published by Henry Holt and Company as How Are you? / ¿Cómo estás?

Copyright © 2018 by Angela Dominguez

All rights reserved. Published by Scholastic Inc., *Publishers since 1920*,
by arrangement with Henry Holt and Company. SCHOLASTIC, SCHOLASTIC EN ESPAÑOL, and
associated logos are trademarks and/or registered trademarks of Scholastic Inc.

The publisher does not have any control over and does not assume any
responsibility for author or third-party websites or their content.

No part of this publication may be reproduced, stored in a retrieval system,
or transmitted in any form or by any means, electronic, mechanical, photocopying,
recording, or otherwise, without written permission of the publisher. For
information regarding permission, write to Henry Holt and Company, LLC,
175 Fifth Avenue, New York, New York 10010.

This book is a work of fiction. Names, characters, places, and incidents are
either the product of the author's imagination or are used fictitiously, and any
resemblance to actual persons, living or dead, business establishments, events,
or locales is entirely coincidental.

ISBN 978-1-338-30646-0

12 11 10 9 8 7 6 5   21 22 23 24

Printed in the U.S.A.   141
First Scholastic printing 2018

How Are You?

¿Cómo estás?

Angela Dominguez

SCHOLASTIC INC.

Welcome!

¡Bienvenida!

¿Cómo estás?

How are you?

Are you hungry?

Are you tired?

No.

¿Estás cansada?

I'm

excited!

Why are you excited?

¿Por qué estás emocionada?

Because I have new amigos!

¡Estamos felices!

¡Fiesta?

Okay!

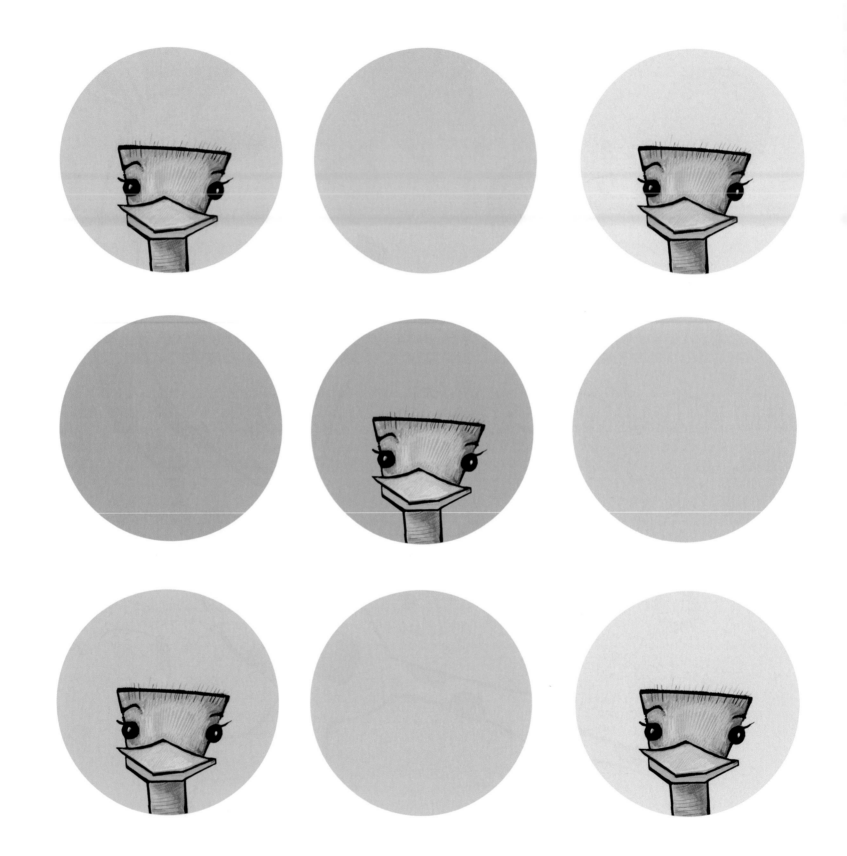

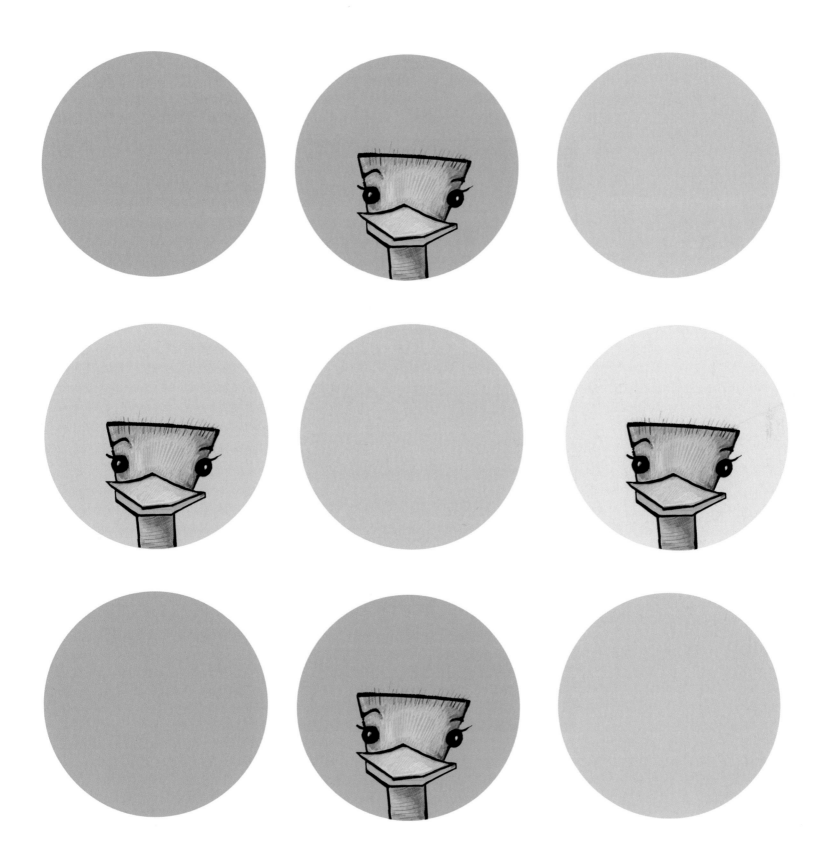

Angela Dominguez writes and illustrates books for children, including *How Do You Say? / ¿Cómo se dice?* and *Maria Had a Little Llama.* She lives in New York City.

Angela Dominguez escribe e ilustra libros para niños, entre ellos se encuentran *How Do You Say? / ¿Cómo se dice?* y *María tenía una llamita.* Vive en la ciudad de Nueva York.

angeladominguezstudio.com